Chocolate Chip

An Urban Tale

Chocolate Chip

JACQUILINE PERRY

TATE PUBLISHING
AND ENTERPRISES, LLC

Acknowledgment

Many thanks to my family and friends who helped me edit and revise this story. Also, thank you to all of the people who have offered their support and have allowed me to practice my writing skills on them.

I hope you enjoy the story as much as I enjoyed writing it.

Contents

Introduction. 9

She Thinks She's Cute 11

Wedding Day Drama 17

Coast to Coast 29

The West Coast. 34

City of Angels. 40

A Storm Is Coming. 45

Happily Ever After 55

Introduction

I woke from a dream that almost seemed like a nightmare. They call me Lady Bug. I was remembering a time when my best friend Chocolate Chip had to grow up practically overnight. She had a great loss in her life and had to walk away from so much more. This was not a dream or a figment of my imagination; it really happened. I learned a lot during that time in my life. It was a time when my eyes opened, and after a while, I learned the subtle differences between holding a hand and chaining a spirit.

> I learned that love should mean security, not envy
> that smiles and kisses aren't contracts,
> And presents aren't promises...
> To build all my roads on today, because tomorrow's ground is uncertain,

And futures can fall in midflight...
I learned, sunshine burns if you bask in
it too long
And get too close,
And after awhile, I learned to plant my
own garden
In order to add fragrance to my soul...
and the world around me.
I learned not to wait for someone to
bring flowers, just grow your own
I learned that you can endure,
You can be strong,
You have worth.
I learned with every good-bye...
You can turn around and say hello.

She Thinks She's Cute

Lady Bug

Chocolate Chip lives in the bricks. She is five feet six with a cream-in-coffee complexion and big brown eyes-dark but light enough to see that they are brown in color. She has a head full of curly jet-black hair. Her voice is soft but strong and determined. When she smiles, her eyes smile too. Everyone tries to get her to laugh because her laugh is infectious.

What makes her special is that she carries herself with complete confidence and is very well-mannered. Chocolate Chip likes to skateboard, to ride her moped, and to play basketball. She is more of a tomboy who happens to be gorgeous. The thing that most impresses me about my godsister is that she is so positive and upbeat regardless of the fact we live in the

projects. Chip is so young, cool, and fresh. She was living in a really nice community just outside the city, but when her mom got hooked on coke, her dad divorced her, and they had to move to "the bricks."

Chocolate Chip was the nickname her mom gave her. Her mom would say, "You remind me of a chocolate chip cookie, and I just want to gobble you up." My nickname is Lady Bug. My friends gave me the name because they say I'm good luck.

Chip's mom was a captain in the fire department. She was caught doing drugs in her work vehicle while on duty and got fired. Her mom tried to get clean. She went to rehab meetings and counseling, but eventually, her dad had to save his daughter. He began a new life in the projects. The projects are public housing. The rent is based on the income and the number of people that one has to support. We call the projects "the bricks."

Chip's father's name was Kingsley, but everybody called him "King." He was a good man. Everyone in the bricks looked up to him. He was a father figure to a lot of the kids. He would hang outside with them and hold court

on current events and hot topics of the city and the world. He knew about a wide variety of topics: community, arts and music, recreation, sports, and, especially, education. As the building supervisor of the neighborhood community center, he was well established in the community already, so the transition back to the hood was not that difficult.

King was at least six feet five. His skin is smooth dark chocolate, and his eyes are light gray that seemed to be endless when you look into them. Chocolate Chip got her smile from him. He was brilliant. He wore his hair in long jet-black locks. Being a dedicated runner made his body muscular and firm. He looked great for his age, so it came as no surprise that on this beautiful spring day in early June, I was in the wedding of Mr. Kingsley Boston and Mrs. Winter Storm Boston.

Winter was a typical project girl. She was handsome rather than beautiful. She was a Ms. Jacquiline beauty product representative and a staff assistant at the local community center. She thought she was so cute. You never saw her unkempt or not groomed meticulously. When she went to the corner bodega, every strand of her hair was in place. She even ironed her underwear. Winter wanted it all. She wanted to be the prettiest, most popular, and most desired in the community. Winter was a proud woman. She succeeded in being the best until Chocolate Chip moved back to the hood. Envy and pride grew more and more in her heart all day and night. Chocolate Chip was beautiful inside and out. Winter was really an ordinary, plain woman, but when she put on her acrylic nails, eyelashes, makeup, and beautiful designer knockoff clothing, she was stunning.

Wedding Day Drama

"Come here, Chocolate Chip," said Winter. "I want you to change into the dress on your bed."

When I saw the dress, I was surprised because it was a different color from the wedding party. In fact it was very colorful. Mine was also really big on me.

Chocolate Chip put hers on and happily glided down the hall and went to the wedding being held in the function room of the community center.

"You look so pretty," Winter said.

Chocolate Chip smiled and said thank you.

I said, "I looked like a piñata filled with candy." That made me giggle.

I was walking around, waiting for the service to begin, when I heard talking coming from a broom closet. Of course, I stopped to listen.

I heard Mrs. Winter talking about Chocolate Chip. She was saying, "Chocolate Chip looks like a fool."

I was startled at how mean she sounded.

Winter said, "She looks like a six-year-old going to a Halloween party." Then she added with a snarl, "If someone sees her outside they would probably give her a treat." She laughed while saying, "She is so skinny and ugly." She then asked the mystery person, "How do I look? Who is the prettiest in here?"

He must have said Chocolate Chip because Mrs. Winter said, "I am going to get rid of her one way or another,"

I heard a man's deep, smooth, baritone sing-song voice say, "She will surpass you."

Just as I was going to bust in, King came up the hall. I couldn't ruin his big day. I couldn't believe my ears. That "witch" was talking about Chocolate Chip. I had to warn Chocolate Chip.

Maybe Winter Storm will stand him up at the altar. She didn't. When the music started to play, I turned around to see her doing the wedding march down the aisle. Winter was wearing a beautiful long wedding gown. It was covered in lace and sparkled with rhinestones. It

looked like a real designer dress. The sight of her made me scared right down to my toes, but I was in awe of her beauty. I looked for Chocolate Chip and spotted her talking to Jadyn Allen, the center director's son. Jadyn was a nice guy. He always has a helping hand for everyone, and he did anything you ask him to. He was truly a gentleman. He knew how to fix bikes, skateboards, and mopeds. Jadyn always was the MC and DJ at all the parties. He could sing and dance. Jadyn did all the music CDs in the bricks, and he did the music for the wedding. The girls were crazy about him.

I started to make my way over to them, but the crowd was too thick. I would have to wait. I glanced at the front of the room to see King looking so nervous but happy. His best friend was standing next to him. As Winter approached him, I thought she was looking at King's best friend with a little smile on her face. Was he the mystery man from the closet? King turned, and I saw him looking at Chocolate Chip, his mouth moving, saying, "Do you have any idea how beautiful you look?" She gleamed with admiration.

"Hi, Lady Bug!" Chocolate Chip said, giggling. "Are you having fun? I am having a great time. Jadyn is so nice. We've been texting back and forth the whole day. He is so funny. Do you think he's cute? He wants to go to see a movie this weekend."

She was going on and on about Jadyn. I did not want to spoil her day by telling her the truth about her stepmom. I decided to wait. Nothing was going to happen until after the honeymoon anyway.

The celebration in the bricks was so festive that evening. The music blasting through the screen doors was a blend of hip-hop, Spanish, and reggae. Kids were playing on the front steps, still dressed in their good clothes. The ice cream truck is screeching its goofy tune. The boys huddled on the basketball court, some playing, some talking trash. The old people just sitting around on their steps were probably discussing the bride and groom. Every little town house was abuzz. In the projects, everyone knows everyone, like in the old days. There is still a sense of community. The adults know all the kids, and the kids know all the adults. There is a strong bond. This is true for all the projects. If you live in a project, all the rest of the people in the project have your back.

A couple of weeks later, I caught up with Chip. She had been sent to her nana's house while her dad was on his honeymoon. She ran up to me and started laughing and smiling, saying, "Jadyn asked me to be his girlfriend. We went to the movies, and when we left, he held my hand. I was so happy because I really like him. Just before he dropped me off at home, he said, 'Look at your text.' When I looked, it said, 'Will you be my girlfriend?' I asked, 'How did you do that? I didn't see you texting.' He said he had it ready to send since the wedding day. Isn't he so sweet? I am going to marry him one day."

"I think you guys are made for each other," I said.

I finally got the chance to talk to Chocolate Chip about what her stepmom said. She was shocked and terrified. She knew I would not make something like that up. She knew this was serious. As long as I have known her, I have never lied to her. Her expression changed, her face became blank. "What should I do? Where should I go? I'm not old enough to legally work. I can't leave Dad, and what about Jadyn?"

"First of all, you need to slow down," I said. "You can go to LA. I have a cousin. His name is Beachman. He runs a co-op for dancers. He is an accomplished artist who is from here. He moved to LA years ago to enhance his work. His brother already lived out there and worked in the movies. I'm sure he could use your help. I'll give him a call.

Chip said, "I always wanted to go to LA."

∽

That evening at dinner, Chocolate Chip spent extra time just talking to her dad about everything. King was so excited to spend the time with his daughter. Winter was annoyed. She finally convinced King to go walk with her up the hill to the bodega. That actually worked out well because it gave Chocolate Chip time to text Jadyn. They texted back and forth for hours as usual. Just before she got tired, she texted that she was going to sleep. Jadyn called and said good-night. He said he wanted to hear her voice to go to sleep. He recited a poem to her.

> I see you inside and out,
> I hear you inside and out,
> I love you inside and out,
> This makes me smile outside and in.

Lady bug and I talked until the wee hours of the morning, setting the plan in motion. I woke up the next morning feeling enthusiastic about everything.

King and Winter were having breakfast when Chocolate Chip went into the kitchen. She began explaining to her dad that she had to go to LA to work with Beachman, who is a great artist and dance instructor, if she was serious about becoming a dancer. King said, "No way." Chip worked on him all morning and even got Nana, her grandma, to call and help. She told him about Gabby Douglas the American Olympic gymnast who had to leave home at fourteen to pursue her dream. She told him the train would only cost one hundred fifty dollars. He said he would talk to Mr. Beachman and buy the ticket today if the conversation with him went well. Winter was happy and helped convince King to let her go. That was when Chocolate Chip realized Winter was glad she was leaving. Winter's whole demeanor changed; she was actually smiling and humming a lot.

The next morning, Chocolate Chip left for LA. King and Jadyn took her to the train station. King gave her a whole list of things not to do on the trip. He gave her a list of phone numbers, a bunch of snacks, and a first aid kit. The first aid kit had not only your standard stuff in it but also other stuff like Vaseline, coupons for Mickey D's and KFC, a Swiss army knife, and an assortment of other interesting stuff. Jadyn gave her a puppy, a toy poodle. She named her Chewy.

When they got to the station, King pulled Chip aside and began a long serious talk about staying focused on education and remaining true to herself. He said to "Live out loud and have fun. Live every day like it is your last." He said to call him every few days and to listen carefully to people before you speak. He went on and on for thirty minutes. Finally he ended it with, "Don't take any wooden nickels."

Chocolate Chip giggled and said, "Dad, what exactly does that mean?"

He explained to her that it means "don't be tricked by the tricksters."

When he was finished, Chocolate Chip had a chance to say good-bye to Jadyn. Jadyn looked so sad. He began by saying, "I wanted to spend every day with you. I am so disappointed that you are leaving."

Chocolate Chip said, "Jadyn, I'll be back before you know it. I will text every day and call often."

He said, "Long distance relationships never work. Absence makes the heart wander."

Chocolate Chip said, "Please be patient for a little while and see if you can come out to LA soon."

Chocolate Chip and Jadyn held hands and talked about the wedding day, the day they got to know each other. They talked about what it means to be girlfriend and boyfriend now. They talked about the distance between them. They talked about looking at the moon at night and wondered if they both would see the same moon.

Jadyn said, "I gave you the puppy so you won't forget me."

With that, tears swelled up in Chip's eyes. Chip knew that she really liked him so much it hurt deeply to say good-bye and she was going to miss someone very special to her. She vowed to herself to always keep him in her heart.

As the train pulled out, Chip's dad yelled, "See you later, alligator."

Chocolate Chip replied, "After awhile, crocodile."

Chewy and Chocolate Chip were off to a new adventure.

Coast to Coast

Chocolate Chip

The trip was going to take about four days with lots of stops. It was the first time I had ever been anywhere. I was scared but excited. The train pulled out at the station heading for New York. I sat next to an older woman who I found out later she use to teach high school english and geography. I thought, *This is sure going to be a boring trip.* I soon discovered it was far from boring. This woman Ms. Jewels knew all the sights.

The next leg of my journey was a 929-mile trip from NYC to Chicago, taking one day. We left Penn Station in Manhattan at about 3:00 p.m. The train traveled alongside the Hudson River. Ms. Jewels told me the name of the body of water I was looking at out my window. I saw a mountain called Storm King Mountain that made me think of Kingsley and Winter Storm. It was famous for being in a movie called *North by Northwest*. I took a picture of it and sent it to my dad. I sent Jadyn a picture of the haunted ruins of Bannerman's Castle located on another island called Pollepel.

After about two hours into my journey, I saw West Point Military Academy. I remembered hearing about this in a movie about the first African American cadet Henry O. Flipper. Ms. Jewel told me all about the story of his court martial and later exoneration in 1999 by President Clinton. It was amazing to see it, although I just mainly saw a mass of green trees and grass.

The train came to a stop in Albany, New York. Chewy and I had a chance to stretch our legs. We normally stop and go out to stretch even if it's just for ten minutes. I saw a guy in the station that seemed to be spying on me or was it just my imagination. Maybe I'm paranoid because of what Lady Bug told me about my stepmom. After a brief stay, we were on our way to Chicago Union Station, home of one of the oldest stations in the country.

Ms. Jewel asked, "Do you want to see Chicago?"

I said yes with so much enthusiasm, I thought she would change her mind. With Chewy in tow, Ms. Jewel and I went to the Skydeck on top of the Sears Tower. From this viewpoint, we could see spectacular views of Chicago and Lake Michigan. I saw the man again. He was tall and dark with a muscular build. He wore a nice pair of Jeremy Scott tennis shoes and a navy-blue Adidas sweat suit. He could have been an athlete once who was now a model.

As we boarded a new train heading to the Pacific coast, I again felt apprehension. I settled in for the 2,438-mile trek. A few hours later, the train rumbled over a bridge that crossed the Mississippi River. We went from Illinois to Iowa and made it officially into the west. I envisioned Huckleberry Finn rafting down the river with his buddy Tom Sawyer. The thought made me wish I had a good book to read. Ms. Jewel must have read my mind because she said, "Would you like to read?" She then pulled a copy of *The Hunger Games* out of her bag. I was overjoyed because I wanted to read that book but wasn't able to get to the library to check it out. "Thank you, yes." I said.

I read for a few hours then pulled out my PSP. I went on the Internet and watched a movie. The next major stop was Denver. We stopped for refueling and servicing. We were 5,280-feet high above sea level. I saw animals that I only saw in picture books and on TV. I thought to myself that Colorado has to be one of the most beautiful places in the world.

When I went to dinner, I noticed the same guy staring at me again. He definitely was eyeing me. As I got off the train at Glenwood Springs, I was told this is where Doc Holiday, a famous gunfighter from the Wild West, spent his last days. Now it is a major recreational center.

Before I knew it, we were going through the scenic Rocky Mountains, Utah, and Nevada. When we got to California, we saw the snow-capped Sierra Nevada Mountains. This is where we had to set are watches back another hour. We traveled through Donner Pass, where some lost hikers had to eat each other to survive. I know I had seen more of America than most Americans, especially the folks in the bricks. I had traveled from the Atlantic to the Pacific. I had made it to the west coast.

The West Coast

I got Chewy and my bag. As I was walking to catch the bus going to LA, I saw the mystery man. He looked like Vin Diesel-tall, well built, and confident. His skin was smooth and creamy. He had a small bit of hair over his top lip, and he looked like he needed a shave. His eyelashes were long, and his eyebrows were dark and thick. His eyes were set back in his face, and his pupils were as large as his irises and jet-black, which gave him a sinister look. He was definitely checking me out. I was positive he was watching me. I made a mental note that I would stay with the group and remain in public at all times. Although I've taken a self-defense class, the possibility of using it for real was scary.

While I was waiting for the bus, I noticed a girl walking around, talking on the phone near me. She didn't have a cart or any luggage at all. I remember thinking, *Why doesn't she go somewhere else and talk on the phone.* It is annoying to hear someone else's conversation. I guess I was feeling a little anxious. My phone rang. I had put the phone in my backpack side pocket so I could maneuver my stuff. I had my jacket draped over the backpack. When I got the phone to answer the call, my coat fell. I picked my coat up and said, "Hello? Hello?" No one answered; it must have been a wrong number. I was only on the phone for a minute. I went to put my phone back in my bag, but the backpack was gone. I started yelling to everyone around to look for the girl with the cutoff jeans, white shirt, and long curly ponytail. Some of the people saw her but not now. She was gone.

My bag had all my important stuff in it-my important papers, my pictures of my dad and Jadyn. I felt so sad and lonely. All of a sudden, the mysterious man with the cool Jeremy Scott's was walking toward me with my bag in his hand. "Does this belong to you?"

I jumped up and scared Chewy when I screamed with joy. The guy told me he found my bag by the newsstand. I examined it and discovered my wallet was the only thing missing. She must have grabbed the wallet and ditched the bag. I guess she did not realize the bag was a North Face.

He said, "My name is Nico Rider." His voice was deep and gruff sounding. I recognized it as the desciption of the man's voice in the closet back at the community center. "I am going to LA to be a police officer. I took the test and passed it. I am accepted in the academy."

Ms. Jewel was staying in San Francisco, so I sure was glad to have a traveling companion for the last six hours of my incredible journey. I said, "Can I hang out with you until we get to LA?"

He said, "That would be great."

As we went past an island, Nico explained, "This was the famous prison called Alcatraz. The prison was notorious for torture and a gangster named Al Capone. But the most interesting thing that happened was the great escape."

"What happened?" I pleaded.

He began by saying, "A very extremely intelligent prisoner nicknamed 'the Bird Man' flew away from Alcatraz."

"What? How?"

"The other prisoners said he saved all of his chicken bones over the years and reconstructed bird wings with them."

I just laughed and laughed. "That is the funniest thing I ever heard. It's impossible!"

He smiled and said, "Then what happened to him? How did he escape?"

I looked over at the island again in wonderment.

City of Angels

I was so amazed when we reached LA. There were palm trees everywhere. The streets looked so clean and manicured, totally different from the East Coast. I just sat at the bus station, trying to think about what to do. I did not have any money. It was stolen. I felt wonderful to be in LA but sad because of my present situation.

Nico must have understood, or he was my guardian angel. He said, "Where are you going, little sis?"

I told him the address. "1958 Cottage Home Street, in the Jungle."

He asked, "The Jungle? Is it in Inglewood?"

"I don't know," I said.

He said, "Come on, kid, I'll take you."

I felt like crying with happiness.

"I think my buddy lives near there," he said. "He lives in the Jungle. That's what they call Inglewood, California."

We took a cab because neither of us knew exactly where we were going. He let me out in front of Beachman's house. Beachman was waiting outside. I called to tell him I was on my way. We introduced ourselves to him and headed inside. Nico said he couldn't stay, but he would come back after he settled in at his friend's house.

༄

Nico called Winter to tell her, "Chocolate Chip is in the Jungle.

Winter said, "I want you to destroy her heart, mind, and soul."

Nico said, "You got it." But as he thought about how sweet and kind Chocolate Chip was, he could not hurt her. When he went to see Chocolate Chip a few hours later, he told her everything and said, "Don't ever go back. Don't call or write. Just disappear, and she may forget about hurting you."

∽

Now I was all alone in the Jungle. I looked around, and everything looked strange. I did not know what to do. I laid on the couch and fell asleep and woke up to an empty, quiet house.

I sat up, looking for Beachman. As I looked around, I saw seven chairs around the table, seven place settings, seven coat hooks, and seven pictures hanging on the wall. When I got up to see if there was something to eat, I saw seven twin-size beds in one of the rooms. I continued on to the kitchen and helped myself to some fruit and veggies. I grabbed a mug and poured some juice. I put the fruit on one of the plates and chowed it down. I took a knife from the table and cut some cheese and bread. After I ate, I went to the room and tried a few beds but fell asleep on the couch in the den.

∽

Later that night, when the occupants of 1958 Cottage Home Street got home, they immediately noticed that someone had been in their house and had also moved and messed with their stuff. They discovered this sweet-looking girl fast asleep on the couch in the den. They did not want to wake her because she looked so peaceful. She was knocked out; she must have been beat.

In the morning when Chocolate Chip awoke, she was scared to death to see all these people staring at her. But they were so kind and friendly, she soon felt at ease. They asked her what her name was. She smiled and said, "Everyone calls me Chocolate Chip." They wanted to know what brought her out to LA all by herself.

She told them her stepmom was jealous of her and wanted to get rid of her. She even sent someone after her. She told them about Nico and how kind he was. The seven guys were a dance crew. They were an aspiring dance troupe. They called themselves the "Sizzling Seven Stars" or S3 for short. They all had nicknames according to their dance moves or style. There was Pop, Twist, Step, Bounce, Boogie, Shake, and Flip. They told Chocolate Chip to "be careful because her stepmom may not give up that easily." They said, "She may send someone to get you. Don't open the door because you don't know anyone in LA."

Chocolate Chip told the Sizzling Seven she would help with the scheduling and the organizing of their gigs. She would keep the place cleaned up, and she would practice her cooking skills on them. Everyone laughed and said thank you. She also explained that she was a dancer and wanted to learn from them. Her dream was to be on *America's Got Talent* or *The X Factor* one day. She was enthusiastic and couldn't wait to work with Paul "Beachman".

A Storm Is Coming

Most of the people were naive to the coming storm. Chocolate Chip called home to talk to her dad, Jadyn, and Lady Bug. She learned that her stepmom was really acting erratic. Winter was always in a rage, acting more diva-ish than her normal behavior.

King said, "She is just going through the empty nest stage of her life, and she miss having you around."

Jadyn said, "I did not notice anything different about her behavior."

Lady Bug on the other hand told Chocolate Chip the real deal. Winter was going around asking everyone how does she look. How is her outfit? Is her hair okay? Insecurities on steroids. She is angry all the time and mumbles about Chocolate Chip constantly.

Lady Bug thinks the motive was ego. Winter wants to be the best and the brightest. She wants to destroy Chocolate Chip. The thought of someone from the bricks other than her being the star was unimaginable. She was becoming the mother crab in the barrel, trying to pull Chip down as she was getting out.

Winter sat around, devising a plan to get Chocolate Chip. She thought and thought how she might destroy her. She realized Nico was not working for her. Chocolate Chip had turned him against her. Envy was driving her mad. Winter was used to people always saying, "You look great. What are you wearing?" Lately all people said was, "How is Chocolate Chip? She is so lovely. She's a star." Winter decided if you wanted something done right, you should just do it yourself. She would disguise herself and pay Chocolate Chip a visit. She dressed up like a really old women. *No one would recognized me*, she thought. She walked through the bricks, and no one knew who she was. In this disguise, she flew to LA. Winter went to the house at 1958 Cottage Home Street in the Jungle. She knocked on the door and pretended to sell Almond Rocha candies. She had poisoned the candies and would seduce Chocolate Chip into eating one.

Chocolate Chip was apprehensive about opening the door, but when she looked out the peephole, she determined that there was no way this sweet little old women could be a threat. She let her in.

Winter said, "You look so frightened."

She said she did not know anyone in LA. The women nodded that she understood. Winter pulled the candies out to let Chocolate Chip sample one. After taking a bite, she immediately fell back on the couch, lifeless.

Winter left and returned to the airport to catch the first flight back to the East Coast. She had risked everything-her life savings, her marriage, and her reputation. If she got caught, it would be jail time for sure, and she would be ruined. To her, it was worth it.

The next day Winter got all dolled up and went to the bodega. Lady Bug ran up to her and asked if she heard the news of Chocolate

Chip. Winter was smiling on the inside. Lady Bug told her how Chip ate something bad and had to go to the hospital. Lady Bug said, "Thank goodness they found her in time. She could have died."

Winter was so mad it looked like smoke actually came out from her head. She yelled out, "Oh my! I haven't heard anything. I need to find King." She cursed and stomped off. Winter was upset but for all the wrong reasons.

Winter was, however, determined to get the job done. When she arrived back home, she immediately began scheming up a new master plan. This time she would tell Nico she had a change of mind about Chocolate Chip. As a token of her new attitude, she would give Chocolate Chip a peace offering. Winter said, "I am going to send her a gift. Can you deliver it?"

Nico said, "Sure."

Winter sent a basket of beauty products. She put the poison in the shampoo. Winter was rotten as a rotten apple.

Flip saw the beauty products as soon as he came home. He grabbed the shampoo and ran to the bathroom. As soon as he opened the shampoo, he smelled it. Apple-pineapple was his favorite. It really didn't matter what the hair product was, he always smelled it. He loved the smell of haircare products. Flip jumped out of the shower, yelling to everyone that something was wrong; that the shampoo smelled stinky. It smelled like almonds and ammonia. Nico knew that it was arsenic poison. Everyone was now on high alert. They had to be extra careful. They did not tell the police they suspected Winter because they weren't positive it was her. They could not accuse King's new wife of attempted murder.

When Winter found out Chocolate Chip was still alive, she tried again. Three strikes and you're out. She got King to send his daughter a basket of fruit as a get-well-soon gift and for being a brave girl. Chocolate Chip was so happy when it arrived; she grabbed an Asian pear, her favorite fruit, and took a big bite. She collapsed to the floor.

That evening when the sizzling seven returned from rehearsal, they found Chocolate Chip lying on the floor, sprawled out, and unconscious, looking dead. They were relieved to see her chest moving, quietly rising and falling. Flip shook her gently but firmly, yelling, "Chip! Chocolate Chip!" She did not open her eyes. They thought she was dead. Her face was a deathly ash. Boogie called an ambulance. Things looked grim. Chocolate Chip looked like she was sleeping. She was in a coma. The sizzling seven all looked angry, ashamed, and full of hurt.

Happily Ever After

At the hospital, they put her in a machine that looked like a newborn's incubator. This was to keep her body temp at 98.6 degrees and her circulation going. Chocolate Chip was not dead but not alive. Chocolate Chip stayed like this for a couple of years. The hospital determined she had a severe allergic reaction to the Asian pear. King was devastated because he had sent the fruit basket. He blamed himself. He was not the same person. He was sad and reclusive.

Jadyn was also miserable. Chocolate Chip was the girl he would love forever. He would move to LA, taking the same route Chocolate Chip took. Initially they wanted to move her back East, but Winter said they just could not afford it. As Jadyn traveled, he remembered the pictures Chip sent him while she was on her journey and smiled at the pleasant memories. People keep telling him "Life must go on." He knows it must, but he was haunted by his feelings for Chocolate Chip. Jadyn finally arrived in LA and had been there a week. It had been two years since he had seen Chocolate Chip. Every day after that, Jadyn would go to the hospital and talk to Chip.

He had been visiting Chocolate Chip for a couple of years when he finally got enough nerve and leaned over and kissed Chocolate Chip on the lips. He was shocked and happily surprised when she opened her eyes and said, "Where am I?"

Jadyn said, "You are with me."

She smiled and said, "I am forever."

He explained everything that happened and then said, "I love you more than anyone or anything else. Will you be my wife?"

Chocolate Chip was still very weak but said with all the enthusiasm she could, "Yes, I will be your wife."

Weeks later, Winter got a card in the mail from LA. She opened it immediately and read, "You are invited to the engagement party of Jadyn Aaron Allen and Zoie Rain (Chocolate

Chip) Boston." This made Winter spin out of control in a rage.

The police investigated her for attempted murder, but they did not have enough proof to arrest her. She was, however, a person of interest. She was shunned by everyone in the community. She proved that envy and jealousy are destructive.

Chocolate Chip, on the other hand, overcame loss and hardship (She had to leave her community, her dad, and her BFF, Lady Bug) because of her strength, kind heart, and inner beauty. Chocolate Chip and Jadyn Allen were engaged and soon received notification that auditions for *AGT* were being held in LA. With the support of Beachman, the Sizzling Seven, King, and Lady Bug, Chocolate Chip set out for the next chapter in her life's story. When one door closes, another door opens. One can only imagine what will happen next.